DASH TO THE R...

by
Jan Fenimore

illustrated by
Vickie Kastl

Doodle and Peck Publishing
Yukon, Oklahoma
405.354.7422
www.doodleandpeck.com

ISBN 978-1-7337170-3-8 (paperback)
ISBN 978-1-7337170-5-2 (hard cover)

Library of Congress Control Number:2019943625

Dedicated to my parents who, by their example, taught me to love books.
JAN FENIMORE

To my husband, Tom, who suffered through an artist with a crashed computer; to my sons, Doug, Patrick, Court, and Craig, who make me proud; to my wonderful grandchildren, Cooper, Chloe, Kyla, Kinsley, Owen, and Lucy, who inspire me; and to my mother, whose loving spirit sustains me still.

VICKIE KASTL

The bitter cold of the Mongolian morning seeped into Dash's bedding. "Brrr. . . I'd better get up and count the animals before Sama takes them to graze."

She pulled on her del. Boru, the family dog, waited patiently. Outside the yurt she found the animals huddled in the hurde (corral). She began her morning count.

Grandfather beckoned her from his yurt. He said, "The worst blizzard of the season is coming. We could lose many animals."

"Grandfather, what can we do?"

Grandfather shrugged. "We'll do what we can."

Back inside the yurt, Mother handed Dash her breakfast yogurt.

Dash's brother, Sama, smiled as he tugged on his boots. "Dash, did you count all the animals this morning? Did we have the same number as last night?"

"You know I count them perfectly every time," said Dash. "I know my numbers. Grandfather says a big storm is coming. You better bring every animal back from grazing."

"Sama," said Mother, "please be careful out there."

Dash heard the noise of an approaching snowmobile. She opened the yurt flap and welcomed her teacher, Mrs. Ersa.

Dash hadn't wanted to attend boarding school like some nomadic children. She loved having her teacher come for lessons three times a week.

Dash handed Mrs. Ersa her essay, entitled "My Favorite Animals." They worked on several pages of math, and read in her science book about cells.

"Good work, Dash," Mrs. Ersa said. "Before I go, pick a story you would like to hear."

Dash found her favorite, the story of Noah. Mrs. Ersa read about Noah building the ark and gathering the animals. Dash pictured them entering the ark, two by two. She smiled when the dove returned, an olive leaf in its beak.

Mrs. Ersa rose to leave. "Time to go. Hopefully, I'll see you in a couple of days."

By late morning the north wind howled. Mother kept the fire blazing inside. Father and Grandfather strapped weather tarps on both yurts. By afternoon, the wind blew the snow sideways.

Sama returned with the animals. Boru followed Dash as she counted them, herding them close for warmth.

"What more can we do?" Father said, as he and Grandfather stood by the fire.

Grandfather said, "We'll leave the dogs outside to keep the animals close. Maybe more will survive."

Suddenly, Dash remembered the story of Noah. "I have an idea. Grandfather can stay in our yurt, and we can put a male and female from each herd in his. We can save at least some of the animals, just like Noah did."

Everyone looked surprised. Sama said, "What kind of crazy idea is that?"

Dash answered, "It worked for Noah!"

"It just might work," Father said. "Someone will need to stay in the yurt to keep them calm."

"Boru and I will stay," said Dash.

Grandfather said, "Let's get busy. Sama, take the dogs and round up male and female horses, sheep, and goats."

By early evening, as the storm raged on, the animals stood, two
by two, in the empty yurt. Dash had moved her bedding to the room's
center so she and Boru could watch them all. The wind howled all night.
Dash and Boru jumped up often to keep the animals still.

By early morning a quiet settled over the camp. Dash left Boru with the animals and went back to her yurt.

"Come, have some hot tea," said Mother. "Father is checking on the other animals. Oh, here he comes now."

Father stomped inside and brushed the snow off his del. "We lost five sheep, two goats and one horse. But thanks to Dash and her Noah story, we will soon be able to add to the herds."

Dash yawned, crawled into her bed, and soon fell asleep...
counting animals, two by two.

AUTHOR'S NOTE

Of the approximately 3 million people who live in Mongolia, almost half of them live and earn their livelihood on the steppes, an area of vast, unforested grassland. As nomads, a people with no permanent home, they travel with their herds of horses, cattle, sheep, goats and camels in constant search of fresh grazing land. The families live off the milk and meat of these animals. The horses, camels and dogs, used for herding, may also share the duties with a motorcycle or a snow mobile.

Some of the children of the nomadic tribes attend a boarding school most of the year. Those families who want to keep their children with them will have a traveling teacher come to where they are several times a week.

Animals freezing during winter is a constant danger. With temperatures well below zero at night, and since the nomads have no place to house their animals, freezing is a real threat.

GLOSSARY

Yurt (yoort)
The structure, also called a ger, is a round, spacious portable structure made of poles which support animal skins or felt made from the wool of the sheep. Most families also own a waterproof covering used in winter or the rainy season. A small, round hole in the top of the yurt, called a toono, allows the escape of smoke. The yurts can be taken down and put up in about two hours. Decorations for the inside of the yurt are colorful and usually, symbols of the culture. The entrance to the yurt always faces south as per tradition and must always be stepped over, rather than on, also by tradition.

Del (del)
Clothing worn by both male and female which consists of a long upper garment and pants of summer or winter weight material. Boots are made of leather with a thick sole and upturned toe. Head gear can be made from a variety of materials, including animal fur or knitted wool.

Hurde (hûrd)
A corral for animals. It is built of wooden poles that can be taken down and moved.

JAN FENIMORE
AUTHOR

Jan Fenimore, an award-winning author and poet, loves reading and writing about indigenous people of the world. After working in middle-school libraries, her desire to educate children about the life and culture of other countries led her to write, *Dash to the Rescue*.

Fenimore lives with her husband at the base of the Sandia Mountains in New Mexico where they enjoy working out, summer concerts at the Bio-Park and the Zoo, and the best of movies year around.

VICKIE KASTL
ILLUSTRATOR

Vickie L. Kastl was born in Central Oklahoma and fell in love with art in second grade after being praised for a drawing of Abe Lincoln. She graduated from UCO with a BA in Education, taught Art and English for thirty-nine years, and was chosen SKIE K20 Innovative Teacher of the Year, and Oklahoma Art Teacher in 1991.

Vickie has illustrated three other picture books. She and her husband travel to collect stories, pictures, and details. She has four sons, five grandchildren and two dogs, Ritchie and Winnie, who pop up in most of her pictures.

DOODLE AND PECK PUBLISHING
YUKON, OKLAHOMA
405.354.7422

www.doodleandpeck.com

Printed in the USA
CPSIA information can be obtained
at www.ICGtesting.com
LVHW070513300723
753625LV00017B/382